The Pieces of Home

The Pieces of Home

by
MISKA MILES

Illustrated
by
Victor Ambrus

An Atlantic Monthly Press Book

BOSTON   Little, Brown and Company   TORONTO

Books by Miska Miles

KICKAPOO

DUSTY AND THE FIDDLERS

SEE A WHITE HORSE

PONY IN THE SCHOOLHOUSE

MISSISSIPPI POSSUM

FOX AND THE FIRE

TEACHER'S PET

RABBIT GARDEN

THE PIECES OF HOME

J
M

ATLANTIC—LITTLE, BROWN BOOKS
ARE PUBLISHED BY
LITTLE, BROWN AND COMPANY
IN ASSOCIATION WITH
THE ATLANTIC MONTHLY PRESS

*Published simultaneously in Canada
by Little, Brown & Company (Canada) Limited*

PRINTED IN THE UNITED STATES OF AMERICA

For Gary Hort

1 Farley's House

FARLEY HAMILTON liked things exactly as they were. He liked his city, his street and his house.

His house was on Filbert Street in San Francisco, and he lived there with his father, his mother, his older brother John, and Chief. Chief was a big black retriever, a very important member of this family.

Their house was narrow and high, with wooden points and circles over the porch along the eaves, and on each side of the door were windows with little panes of glass the color of cranberry jelly.

If you stood outside, looking in, everybody looked red. And if you were on the inside, looking to the outside, it looked as though the world were on fire.

Farley liked the rooms in this house; rooms that went back in a row to a small garden with a

willow tree, and to the stairs that led almost straight up to the room he shared with John.

He liked all the things that were there; his own phonograph with its big red horn, and John's American flag that hung against the wall.

Then, there were other advantages to having a house in San Francisco. There was Golden Gate Park. There was Fisherman's Wharf. And best of all, there was Chinatown.

4

If he followed his own street a little way and angled right, he was soon on Dupont Street in Chinatown.

This particular Saturday morning Hong came from Chinatown with the vegetables.

Sometimes he came with a small cart and a bony black horse, but today he shuffled up the street, carrying two baskets slung from the ends of a pole balanced across his shoulder. His cone-shaped hat shielded his face from the mist of the fog.

"Hong's here," Farley shouted.

Hong climbed the back steps and set the baskets on the kitchen floor. "Bad day, good vegetables," he said.

Mrs. Hamilton looked in the baskets. "Get back, Chief." Chief sat down and thumped a welcoming tail against the linoleum floor. "The carrots look nice," Mrs. Hamilton said, "and the lettuce."

Farley reached for a big white cup and poured into it the last of the breakfast coffee which was

5

always kept hot for Hong on vegetable day.

"Bad day," Hong repeated.

"It does look a bit darker than usual. Perhaps it will storm." Mrs. Hamilton added a red cabbage to the vegetables she had chosen.

"I remember a day like this," Hong said. "I come from China and big monster swallowed the sun. Day was dark and sea gulls went to sleep. All year bad."

"What you saw was probably an eclipse of the sun," Mrs. Hamilton said. "The moon's shadow crossed the sun."

"Maybe so. Maybe not," Hong said. He reached into his basket and pulled out presents of white coconut candy and nuts. "Pretty soon now, Chinese New Year, you come Chinatown." He held the cup between his hands and sipped happily. "You see parade. You see dragon Wong Fong."

Farley thought about the monster that swallowed Hong's sun. That seemed more exciting than thinking about an eclipse. And who knows maybe something *would* happen when the day was dark and glowering and quiet and strange like this day.

He put on his cap and went outside. Chief pushed outside with him. Farley stood on the back porch leaning against a post, and after a while, lightning zigzagged across the sky, and thunder rolled and the earth seemed to rock. Farley watched the rain pour down. Well, a good

7

old thunderstorm was nothing to get excited about.

"Unusual weather," his father would say.

Thunder cracked sharply.

Sounds like a string of firecrackers, Farley thought.

He called to John. "Hey John. Why don't we go to Chinatown and buy firecrackers?"

They sloshed along Dupont Street, heading straight for the sausage shop in Chinatown.

Everyone was getting ready for New Years. In the street the merchants were painting their signs

with gold paint. There were lanterns and big
butterflies made of silver-colored paper, and people called to each other. Their words sounded
like temple gongs.

"Cantonese sounds like singing," John said.

Many of the men carried packages and big
bunches of sweet-smelling narcissus.

In the sausage shop Farley laid his money on
the counter. "I want ten cents worth of firecrackers," he said.

The shopkeeper wrapped the firecrackers in
brown paper.

9

Outside, the boys ambled slowly along the narrow street. The rain had stopped. Farley always found things in the shopwindows to admire: flattened dried sea horses, little shriveled frogs. He could think of a lot of uses for little shriveled frogs. There were pig livers too, dull as shoe leather, and dried fish skins, shining purple and pink as the inside of an abalone shell. There were live snails and white piles of candied coconut strips.

They stopped in front of a Chinese laundry.

Ironing boards were set up inside, and men in blue cotton trousers and jackets pushed the irons back and forth.

Five men worked in the small room which was open to the street, where any passerby could stop and watch. Shirts and great white tablecloths and wide petticoats were spread over their boards, and beside each ironer was a beautiful big bowl.

As Farley and John watched, one man folded a shirt and reached for another. Carefully he spread it on his board.

He stooped over his bowl, a big yellow bowl
decorated with sprays of purple and green flow-
ers. He filled his cheeks with water from the
bowl, and whoof — it was huffed out in a fine
spray that sprinkled the shirt. It was ready for
ironing.

Much better than the way his mother sprinkled
with her fingers, Farley thought. They walked
on to the corner and stopped to let a fish peddler
pass by. His old gray horse clopped slowly along
in the direction of Fisherman's Wharf.

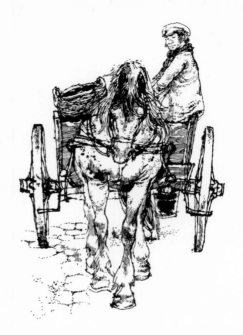

In the back of the wagon, a tall, empty basket
tipped against the tail gate and toppled into the
street.

"Hey," Farley yelled. "Hey." He picked up
the basket and sprinted to catch up with the
wagon. "You dropped a basket."

The fish peddler stopped his horse and waited
while Farley tossed the basket into the wagon.
The man slapped the reins against his horse's
rump and moved out of the way of an oncoming
cable car.

John tugged his cap forward. "I'll treat you to a ride home," he said.

On the way home Farley was tempted to open his package, twist off a few firecrackers and shoot them off from the car. But he had no match and thought better of the idea.

At home he put them in a tin box to save for a special occasion. He pressed the lid on tightly.

2 *Chinese New Year*

THEN IT WAS Chinese New Year.

Farley and John walked along Dupont Street, and firecrackers were popping in the gutters. The air smelled salty with powder smoke. Farley looked up at the balconies from which dripped long strings of red and yellow firecrackers. Bright paper lanterns hung in every doorway.

The boys walked slowly and became part of the crowd that was dressed in the colors of the

14

peacock — blue and gold, green and purple. They breathed deeply of the pork cooking in braziers set in open windows.

When Chinese met Chinese, each clasped his own hands together and bowed above them. Each called a happy greeting to the other in singing Cantonese.

A package of firecrackers exploded close by, and a cat came streaking along the sidewalk. A girl followed calling loudly.

"She'll never catch it," John said, and as he spoke, Farley reached down and he had it — twisting in his hands.

It was a spotted cat with a tail like a question mark. "Is this your cat?" he asked the girl.

"It is mine," she answered.

"It hates the noise," Farley said.

The girl took the cat and held it closely. It pushed its head under her arm. The girl waited there and Farley didn't know what to say to her.

John spoke. "Are you waiting for someone?"

"I am waiting for my father and my brothers. The cat and I ran away from them." She smiled up at John.

After a while her father came, matching his pace to the steps of her three small brothers, and they all went slowly along the street.

Farley looked at them curiously. They were all dressed alike in the familiar wide trousers and loose coats with sleeves that came down over their hands, but the fine silk clothing of the father was dark while his children were gay in purple and green.

The family turned into a doorway. Farley wondered why the Chinese men wore long braids hanging limply against their backs, and he had a glimpse of an open door.

"That's where they live. Up those stairs," Farley said. For a moment he thought about the advantages and convenience of living in Chinatown, and then discarded the idea in favor of his own house on Filbert Street.

He looked at the shopwindows, close-shuttered

for the holiday. Above, the girl was at a window,
but she didn't look down. She leaned out, watching along the street—waiting for the parade.

Now, people were meeting at the curb. Chinese
and their visitors crowded together, and Farley
knew they wouldn't have long to wait for Wong
Fong the dragon.

Finally he heard the beating of gongs.

18

"Here he comes!" Farley shouted. "Look! The dragon!"

Drums beat and people called out and down the street came the dragon master, waving his staff.

Cavorting behind him were blue-denim legs, dozens of legs dancing beneath the body of the dragon, that great horned beast of bamboo and silk, hung with tiny mirrors and jewels of all colors—glittering—dazzling.

On it came. It writhed and twisted and breathed fire and smoke, and those who supported its body yelled like a million demons, and Farley yelled too.

The dragon passed by and then came the parade of the people.

Following were the merchants and the bankers, the men from the telephone company and the gas company, the laundrymen and the man from the sausage shop. Then there was Hong, and Farley waved and shouted and Hong waved back. They were carrying fat paper lanterns, and behind them were women and children.

The parade was over and the crowd was thinning.

"I wish we could stay," Farley said.

"I know," John said. "Their New Year's party is just beginning. But that's for them. We have to go." He reached in his pocket. "I've got carfare. Let's ride."

20

They waited for the cable car. People were calling to each other and bowing. Farley and John sat outside on the car where they could watch the excitement along the street. The wind blew from the bay and two sea gulls flew low overhead and their gray shadows crossed Farley's knees.

Back on his own front porch, Farley looked through the cranberry glass. Everything inside looked glowing and warm. When they opened the door, Farley smelled apple pie. He went straight through the house to the kitchen. He took a deep breath and was glad to be home.

"How was the parade?" his mother asked.

"The dragon was a block long," Farley said. "Everybody threw money on it, and the boys underneath humped the dragon's back up and down and all the money fell off and everybody grabbed for it. Golly, it was fun."

And then, it was April.

With homework to do, Farley and John sat at the big round table in the dining room. Farley hooked his feet over the chair rungs and reached for his tablet. He had ten arithmetic problems to figure out. He wet the end of a pencil and tackled the first one.

Finally, after studying for what seemed to be weeks, the clock called the time. Farley jumped to his feet. "Nine o'clock," he said.

"And bedtime," said his father.

Farley went to the kitchen door and whistled for Chief, who came plunging up the steps. He led the way upstairs and flopped down beside the bed.

Farley felt pleased that his arithmetic paper was ready for school tomorrow.

He pulled off his pants and shirt and under-clothes and laid them over a chair. Quickly he slipped on his nightshirt and hopped into bed.

John turned off the light.

Farley lay there without moving until his eyes were accustomed to the dark. He could hardly see the outlines of the familiar things in the room —bookcase—chairs.

It seemed unusually dark and still this night, and Farley thought of Hong and hoped that his monster had not swallowed the moon.

It seemed that the only noise in the world was the howling of a dog somewhere and the sound of a foghorn in the distance.

He shut his eyes.

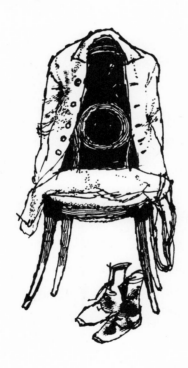

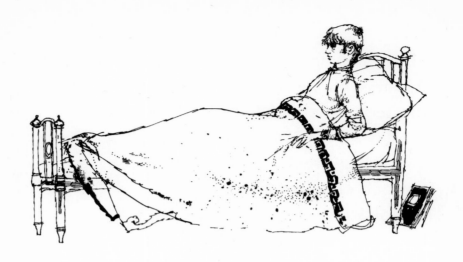

3   The First Day

FOR SOME frightening reason Farley awakened when the clock in the kitchen called out the hour of five.

Day was coming through the window and at his side, John slept soundly, his breathing deeply peaceful.

Farley lay there unmoving, almost as though he waited for something. Far off, he heard the whinny of a horse, and beside the bed, Chief growled.

Then it happened.

From somewhere out over San Francisco came a deep roar and rumble like the sound of guns fired from the cliffs. And the bed was sliding, slowly sliding across the room, as if it were pushed from wall to wall by an unseen hand. Farley sat upright.

"Wake up." Farley could hardly get the words out. Then his voice grew strong. *"Wake up, everybody."*

Their father shouted from the hall. "Get up! Get up! There's an earthquake. Get outside."

"Chief's under the bed and won't come out," Farley said. His teeth chattered as though he were cold. The bed had gone to rest against the far wall. At the moment he stooped to coax the dog from under it, it lurched aside and Chief jumped to his feet and looked wildly around.

Farley reached for the doorknob, which jerked away to one side as though to escape his touch. He lunged for it again. He tried to steady himself against the tipping wall. He caught the knob and the door opened. The three crowded down the

25

rocking stairs. Like Crazy House, Farley thought.

Outside, in their nightclothes, the family stood together in the middle of the street.

In the first light of morning, the embroidered ruffle on the neck of her nightgown showed white above his mother's dark bathrobe. Her long hair was caught with a small ribbon.

The earth still shook, and all along the street neighbors called to each other.

"What should we do?"

"Look, your chimney's down."

"It moved my kitchen stove clear across the room."

"What will we do? Where will we go? What will happen?"

And when the earth quieted they called out almost apologetically:

"Is it over?"

"How will we know when it's over?"

"Look at our front steps. They've been shaken away from the house."

Then the earth shook again and again, and all

along the street the people waited fearfully —
almost too afraid to talk. Church bells rang
where no hand pulled the bell rope. Finally there
was quiet.

"Look," Farley said. "There goes Chief.
Chief." Farley started out after him.

"Farley." His father's voice came to him like

thunder. "Farley. Come back here. Let that dog go."

"But the earth's cracking open," Farley said. "Chief might fall in."

"Don't be ridiculous," Father shouted. "Come back here. He'll come back. He knows where home is."

Reluctantly, Farley returned.

Suddenly he was conscious of running around in his nightshirt. "I want to get dressed," he said. "I'm going to get my pants on."

"Ask your father if you can go in the house," his mother said. "You'll stay out here until he says it's safe to go inside. I think we should *all* stay here. The roof could fall in."

"There's no danger of that," Father said. "Frame houses yield with the shaking. I'll go inside and look. You stay here. You, too, Farley."

He went up the steps and tried to open the door. The house had settled against it. He leaned with his shoulder and the door jerked open.

It seemed that he was gone a long time. Farley

stood first on one foot and then on the other. He watched the small clusters of people along the street and listened to their hushed, frightened voices.

"Golly, Farley," John said. "I hope your new record wasn't broken."

Their father appeared at the door. "It's bad in here—but I think it's safe," he said.

Farley took the steps two at a time.

In the front room a small table was overturned and a vase was broken. The pictures on the wall were askew, and the chairs had slid together in one corner. Like somebody having a meeting, Farley thought. He went on.

In the dining room the top of the sideboard had crashed to the floor and with it, the glassware on it. Beyond, in the kitchen, cupboard doors were flung wide and their shelves emptied on the floor. A large calendar had fallen from its hook.

Farley replaced it and he looked at the clock.

"Clock stopped at thirteen minutes after five," he said.

He hurried upstairs.

Everything seemed to be all right except for the bookcase which was overturned.

He looked for a box of records and carried records and phonograph down to the dining room and set them on the table.

He put on a record and wound the crank.

For half a minute he listened to the music, "Meet me in St. Louis, Louis—" accompanied by a rhythmic, regular click.

"Turn that thing off," his father called from the kitchen.

"Okay," Farley said. "I just wanted to see if my new record was cracked and it is."

In the kitchen his mother lifted a lid from the stove and touched a match to the paper under the kindling.

"Don't do that." Instantly Father was beside her, grabbing paper and kindling from the stove and dropping them into the coal bucket. "John. Water. A fire in the stove might set the house afire. Our chimney is probably cracked through. John."

"I'm trying. There isn't any water," John said.

"The faucet's wide open. And only a drop came out."

"Never mind. I think everything's all right here. But just to be sure give me the salt."

Farley handed the salt box to his father who emptied it into the stove.

"Well," said Mother, "if I can't cook, what do we eat?"

Farley picked up an unopened package of cornflakes from the floor.

"Farley's found breakfast," John said. "Hey Farley, what about finding a can of milk?"

There was a bang on the back door.

"That's Chief," Farley said. He opened the door to let him in.

After they had eaten, Father put on his suit and picked up his derby and settled it on his head. "I'm not at all sure there'll be any business today. It depends on what damage was done downtown. I'll go along and take a look at Market Street."

"I'll go too," Farley said.

His father hesitated. "There may be school today. Perhaps the damage is confined to this area."

"But maybe there won't be school," Farley said.

"Well, come along," Father said. "John?"

Mother spoke before John could answer. "One of you will have to stay here. I don't want everybody to go."

"Okay," John said. "Let Farley go. I'll stay here with Mother."

4   *Downtown*

FARLEY and his father walked together along the street. Almost every brick chimney along the way was down. Some of them had crashed to the sidewalk, some were sheared off and had fallen to the roofs. When Farley and his father reached Market Street, they walked in the middle of the street, for the sidewalks were covered with glass and plaster.

"It's worse than I expected," Father said.

In the distance, wisps of black smoke reached upward. "Look," Farley said. "I see smoke." He thought of the empty water tap at home. "I hope

34

there's water in the hydrants to fight the fire
with."

"I hope so, too," his father said. "Indeed I
do."

Even as his father spoke, Farley heard the
gongs of a fire engine, and there, coming from
the side street, three great horses plunged into
the intersection, their hoofs striking hard against
the cobblestones. A fireman held fast to the reins,
and others stood on the back platform, hanging
on as they swerved around the corner. Black
smoke poured from the stack.

"Look at them go." Farley shouted.

His father shook his head. "I wonder what they will do if there's no water."

Avoiding the rubble, Farley and his father went on. Refugees from Chinatown crossed their path.

Farley heard one man say to another, "Almost every building in Chinatown has been destroyed or badly damaged."

"Father," Farley said. "Did you hear what the man said?"

His father nodded. "Most of the buildings there were made of bricks," he said.

Farley watched these quiet people as they filed past: the homeless, carrying something to remind them of what had been — a canary in a cage, a pot of narcissus, a bronze vase.

He thought of the things in his own home; his phonograph, his baseball mitt, things he'd had for a long time—his collection of lead soldiers.

They walked around the ruins of a fallen wall and Farley looked up into rooms exposed to the street like those of a primitive cliff dwelling.

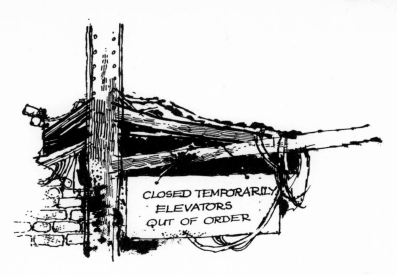

Someone had put up a sign: CLOSED TEM-
PORARILY. ELEVATORS OUT OF ORDER.

"Somebody's idea of a joke," Farley said.

They walked around and over the fallen debris.
Father's office was a framework of steel.

Four soldiers went by. They carried rifles with
bayonets and canteens hung from their belts.

"I'm glad to see the men from the Fort,"
Father said. "In an emergency such as this there's
bound to be lack of discipline. With the soldiers
here, we'll have order."

Another fire engine rolled past, gongs ringing
and horses snorting. Smoke rose high from the
buildings south of Market Street.

Someone shouted that the Opera House had fallen. Everywhere there was splintered wood, and buildings creaked. The smoke lay low, pungent and heavy.

"We'd better start for home," Father said.

When they reached home, Mother was waiting on the porch. "Was it bad?"

"Very serious." Father put his arm across her shoulder. "From now on, we all stay together. If the fire reaches our block we'll have to leave."

"Shall we start packing?" Mother asked.

"No," father said. "It's still safe here. We won't leave unless we have to."

Finally night came, and the sky glowed softly pink and gray.

"We'll sleep outside," their father said.

Farley helped drag mattresses outside and carried quilts to heap on them.

All along the street, people spread their blankets on the ground, and fully clothed, lay down to sleep.

Farley slept fitfully and dreamed of a fire coming upon him like a dragon breathing yellow flames, and even as he dreamed, he smelled smoke, heavy and sharp.

In the night when he awakened, he heard strangers going by — walking — walking — and it was with a feeling of strange excitement that he thought of the fire creeping closer and closer.

San Francisco was burning.

He thought of this home and the things that were part of it: the willow tree, beneath whose branches he had gone to hide since he could re-member; of the attic where there were trunks filled with funny old clothes and brittle letters; of his own new baseball glove and his set of regular carpenter's tools.

Perhaps the fire won't come this far. Perhaps there will be rain.

He looked at the sky, and through a mist of smoke, the stars twinkled.

5   The Second Day

FARLEY AWAKENED early and called the others. He was almost sure that the fire was near.

"I am awake," Father said. "There is plenty of time. Plenty. Where is the list of things we will take?"

"Right here," Mother said. "I have everything ready to go in the basket."

John hurried to get the big laundry basket.

"We'll take dishes," his mother said. "At least we'll take the plates and cups and saucers that weren't broken." She touched the big blue and white soup tureen and her fingers followed its curve. "We can't take the big pieces."

"We can use one of the blankets to pack the

dishes in," John said. "And I'll roll up the rest of the bedding. Farley can carry his share."

Farley allowed John to fasten a roll of bedding against his back. He thought of something and ran awkwardly toward the stairs.

"You're not supposed to run with a pack like that," John said.

Farley hunted around upstairs in the bedroom until he found the firecrackers he'd bought in Chinatown. He tucked them in the center of his bedding roll and hurried back down.

Father was checking the weight of the basket. "There are enough tents set up in Golden Gate Park for every family that will need one," he said. He opened his jacknife and went outside.

He returned with a length of clothesline and made a rope collar for Chief.

Farley looked at the rope. "That ought to hold him," he said.

There was pounding on the door.

A soldier stood outside. "Time to go," he said. He sounded tired.

"We're ready," Father answered.

Farley looked at his mother. She was dressed in her street costume, a long dress with puffed sleeves. She wore gloves and a feathered hat and she looked very stylish. But she had a smudge across her face.

Chief tried to shake his rope collar, but Mother held him in check. She smiled at Farley. "You're looking at my dirty face, aren't you? I couldn't use water for washing. I put what we had in your father's canteen, and that's for drinking."

They were ready to go. Farley lifted his side of the basket. His father and mother led the way. Mother held tightly to Chief's collar and carried the cuckoo clock.

Father had a satchel. "Full of important things," he said. "Insurance papers. The deed to our land."

"And the silver," Mother said.

"And if you think it isn't heavy," Father said, "I'll trade loads."

"What will we do if the fire burns the tents?" Farley asked.

Father answered quickly. "There are hundreds of acres there. There is nothing to worry about. The park is a natural firebreak."

Farley knew that his mother was trying not to cry. He glanced at John. John was looking straight ahead, holding the phonograph horn under one arm.

"Hey," Farley said. "What are you doing with my horn? You can't use the horn without the phonograph box, you know."

"I know," John said. "The box is in the basket. With records."

Farley felt pleased about this and wished that he had thought to do something for John.

His father had taken his mother's arm.

"A carload of food came in last night from Los Angeles," he said. "Everything will be all right."

A man and a woman hurried to pass. The man pushed a trunk supported by two pairs of roller skates. The woman carried a washboard.

"What's she got the washboard for?" Farley asked.

His father waited until the man and woman were a distance ahead. "Haven't you noticed what strange things people save when they're excited? Look at us. Mother has a clock. John has a phonograph horn, and you, Farley, have a roll of something in your pocket."

"I brought the calendar," Farley said. "It seemed like a good idea to know what day it is." He thought about school and wondered what had happened to the things in his desk. He wondered what happened to ink when a schoolhouse burned.

"We're all acting as though we aren't going back," Father said. "Remember, they may get the fire under control at any minute. It may never reach our house. We may go back and find everything just as it was."

"And if we don't?" Mother asked.

Farley answered. "We'll just have to start over together and build another house."

46

From the way his father looked back at him Farley knew that this was the right answer.

People still streamed along the streets. A few lucky families had their belongings stacked high in carts drawn by sleepy-looking horses.

"A horse would certainly come in handy about now," Farley said.

"You've walked this far many times," Father said. "Without a heavy load, of course. That makes a difference. I can carry awhile, if you are tired."

They set the basket on the ground and John changed sides. Finally, ahead was the green of the park. Mother released Chief, who ran ahead. Farley tried to run too, stumbling, almost falling. He looked at the tents and the relief workers, and suddenly everything seemed ordered and secure.

He sat down on the ground. Somebody was taking care of everything. There was even a big blackboard for the name of anyone who was separated from his family.

Farley slipped his arms out of the ropes that

held his own pack, and he stretched out on the ground, smelling the earth. He lay there, waiting.

And then his family had arrived and they were being shown to a tent.

"How nice," Mother said. "A tent all to ourselves."

Farley was watching the unpacking when he heard a disturbing noise.

He dashed out of the tent and followed the sound. He came upon a girl about his own age. She was sitting under an oak tree and she was sobbing bitterly.

Farley looked closely. He thought he had seen her before. He watched for a while, but she didn't look up. Finally he spoke.

"Hey. Why are you crying?"

She didn't answer.

"Did your house burn?"

She shook her head. He watched her tears as they rolled down her cheeks and spread out on her purple coat. She was the girl from Chinatown.

"You're the girl with the cat," Farley said.

6   *The Girl with the Cat*

"YOU'RE THE GIRL with the cat," Farley said again. "You have to stop crying. Stop."

Obediently, she pushed at her face with her sleeves.

"When the earth shook, there was such noise that my cat ran away. I couldn't find her when we left. She's lost. And now I'm lost too. I can't find my mother or my father or my brothers."

"How did you get to the park?"

"We came together, but now I can't find them."

"I'll write your name on the blackboard," Farley said. "You can stay with us until they find you. What's your name?"

"Su-Mei—"

He added a line to the list on the board.

FOUND: SU-MEI. LOOK IN FARLEY HAMILTON'S TENT.

In front of the tent Farley's mother was cooking over a small stove.

"Look what I found," Farley said. "Her name's Su-Mei. She's lost."

"We can put her name on the blackboard," his mother said.

"I did."

Mother put her arms around Su-Mei and looked at Farley intently. "Every now and then you surprise me," she said, "and pleasantly."

Farley felt good. He wondered if he might have grown an inch or two.

His mother looked at the sun. "It's almost noon. I wonder if Su-Mei would like to help me fix dinner?"

Farley sat under a big buckeye tree and watched Su-Mei working with his mother. He wondered if Su-Mei's cat had stayed near its home in Chinatown. Cats were like that, he knew. He wished it weren't such a long way back. He would like to look for the cat.

After they had eaten their noonday meal, Far-

ley sauntered over to a path that led to the main tent where supplies were kept. He smelled fish. There was the old gray horse and the wagon that belonged to the fish peddler from Chinatown. When the baskets were empty, the peddler climbed back to the seat and picked up the reins.

"Are you going for more fish?" Farley asked him.

The peddler looked at him and a big smile spread across his face. "I go for more fish."

"Can I ride with you?"

"You can ride."

Chief came trotting up. "But you can't come,"

Farley said. "You stay here. Stay. I'm on cat business."

He stepped on the hub of a wheel and climbed up to the seat. He had never been in a fish peddler's wagon before. It smelled like crab. This was a strange day, a day of freedom when everyone was so busy that no one paid attention to one boy.

They rode north away from the burning, and crossed toward the bay. Then there, just a bit to the right, was Fisherman's Wharf.

Farley looked at the red sails of a boat that rocked at the wharf, and he watched while a fisherman helped the peddler load his wagon with fish.

"Everybody helps today?" the fisherman asked. "Even the boy?"

"I'm hunting for a cat," Farley said. "I came because I need a piece of bait."

The fisherman handed him a piece of squid. "I have heard of bait for fish," he said, "but never for cat."

When the baskets on the wagon were filled with fish, the peddler picked up his reins.

"I'll get off at Dupont Street," Farley said.

Chinatown as he had known it was gone. Tops of buildings were shorn off as though a giant's hand had swept across them. Farley went straight to the corner where Su-Mei's family had turned in at their own doorway. There were neither people nor animals in sight, unless you counted the soldier in the next block. Farley wondered if the soldier would stop him. He wished he'd gone on with the fish peddler. Maybe he'd better duck out of sight.

Then he saw the cat.

It was a spotted cat with a tail like a question mark. It crouched beside the sidewalk ready to run.

He stooped and called softly: "Here, kitty-kitty-kitty." It doesn't understand English, Farley thought. He held out a piece of squid. The cat stretched its neck forward and flattened its stomach against the earth. It was hungry —

Farley laid the squid on the ground and the cat reached for it. Farley made a desperate grab and he had the cat. He held it securely in the crook of his elbow.

He hurried on to his own house. Pieces of cranberry glass lay scattered on the porch. He picked up a piece and put it in his pocket.

He hurried around the house to the willow tree. He felt so good that he wondered what he might get for John.

He thought of John's flag — he'd get the flag to remind John of all that had been in this house.

He carried the cat up the back steps and on upstairs to his old bedroom. The bedroom was warm. He didn't dare set the cat down. He reached for the flag with his left hand and hurried down the stairs.

In the dining room the big tureen stood in its usual place on the sideboard where his mother had left it. He wondered how he could manage flag and cat and soup tureen at the same time. Then he knew what he could do.

The tureen was big and the cat was small, and the place where the spoon rested against the lid would let in plenty of air. He put the cat in the tureen and slid on the heavy cover.

"I know you won't like being in that soup bowl," Farley said. "But it won't be for long, and you're safe."

He picked up the flag and propped the staff in his side pocket and it rested comfortably against his shoulder. He picked up the tureen with the cat inside.

When he opened the door, he saw a soldier coming across the street. "Look, you," the soldier called. "You're looting. You're old enough to know better than that. Put that stuff back where you got it."

"But—" the words stuck in Farley's throat. "This is ours."

"I've heard that before," the soldier said. "Put it back."

Farley retreated into the house and ran through the kitchen and out the kitchen door. The cat meowed pathetically.

Farley took one last look at the willow tree. It looked thirsty and its boughs reached down and touched the troubled earth.

7 *In the Park*

WITHOUT making any more noise than he could help, Farley climbed through the fence into the next yard and on through the one beyond until he reached the side street.

A bay horse and a spring wagon were coming along the street. The wagon was piled high with belongings. A driver slapped the reins against the horse's back.

"Would you give me a ride, Mister, please?" Farley called. The driver stopped his horse.

"What have you got there?"

"I've got my mother's soup bowl," Farley said. "I've been home." The cat meowed. "And I've got a couple of other little things. Our house is just around the corner from here."

"I suppose you're going to the park?" the man asked.

"Yes sir."

"Climb up," the driver said.

At the park Farley slid down from the wagon. "Thanks for the ride." As he crossed toward his tent, the cat set up a plaintive wailing, and Chief leaped high in the air to get at the tureen.

"Hold him, somebody," Farley said. "I've got Su-Mei's cat." He saw that Su-Mei's family had found her.

"And the flag," John said. "You got the flag —"

"Take it." Farley twisted to the side so John could reach the staff. Then Mother saw Farley.

"Farley. You didn't. You went back. You knew I wanted that."

"Careful," Farley said. "I've got a cat in it. Su-Mei, here's your cat." He looked at his mother. "I found it in the gutter right by her house. Down, Chief. Let him smell the cat and he'll be all right. Good dog. Good cat. There. Now he's all right. Good dog."

Chief yawned and scratched at his rope collar.

"Oh Farley," Mother said, "what a boy."

John came with a bowl of tinned milk and set it on the ground and Su-Mei sat close by and they all smiled to hear the loud and happy purring of the cat.

Mother touched Farley's shoulder. "Our house? Is the fire closer?"

Farley nodded. He had a strange and lonesome feeling, for he knew that he had looked at their house for the last time. His mother turned away, and after a while he followed her into the tent.

Someone had set the clock. Its pendulum swung back and forth and his calendar was pinned to the side wall. He felt in his pocket for a pencil and circled the date of the earthquake, "April 18, 1906," he said. He took out his piece of cranberry glass and polished it on his pants.

When evening came they all stood in the bread-line for food: Farley, his parents, John, Su-Mei and her family. Su-Mei held her cat.

"Supplies are coming by train," Father said. "Fresh meat and potatoes. I understand that box-cars of food are arriving from all over the United States."

Everybody cared about San Francisco. It made Farley feel warm and good.

Afterward they took their provisions back to

the tent and Farley watched while supper was prepared. He thought about homes — his house on Filbert Street — the tent in Golden Gate Park.

On the third day the fire still burned. Even at three o'clock in the afternoon fire joined fire and swept down to the sea.

Farley watched the people still going past, carrying their pets, their belongings — walking — walking.

Finally on this day, soldiers rode through the park calling out that the fire was under control.

After supper Farley put a record on the phonograph, and he and John and their mother and father, sat quietly while they listened. They were together just as they had been on Filbert Street.

Chief, his tail wagging, trotted across the park. He's looking for a handout, Farley thought.

That night when Farley lay down to sleep, the box of firecrackers made a pleasant lump under his blankets.

Chief pushed in under the flap of the tent and flopped down beside Farley.

"I'm glad you're home," Farley said.

Date Due

OC 16 '70					
NO 21 '74					
FEB 27 '78					
MAR 2 '78					